My Princess Collection

Ariel

A Gift of Love

Book Twelve

For more Disney Press fun,
visit www.disneybooks.com

Chapter One

Welcome to Atlantica. I'm Princess Ariel. I'm a mermaid, but my father, King Triton, has a magic trident that can transform me into a human! It's as a human that I now live with my husband, Prince Eric, in our palace on dry land.

My father always told me to stay away from humans, but I was so curious about them.

One of my favorite things to do was to explore sunken ships. My best friend, Flounder, and I found the most wonderful human treasures inside them.

Daddy said humans were cruel. But I knew that any creature who could make things as beautiful as those treasures couldn't be all bad.

Chapter Two

One day, I found something amazing. Back then, I didn't know anything about the human world. But our friend Scuttle, the seagull, did. He told us it was a "dinglehopper"—and that humans use it to comb their hair.

Then, Flounder and I swam to a secret cave where I kept my human treasures. I turned on a music box and watched the tiny couple inside dance. I wished I could dance and be part of the human world.

Flounder and I were arranging my treasures when a ship passed overhead. We swam up to take a look.

Suddenly, a storm blew in. Powerful waves pushed the ship closer to the rocks near the shore! Then, the human they called Prince Eric fell overboard! I dove underwater to rescue him, and I was able to pull him to shore. I had never been that close to a human before. Eric

was very handsome. I couldn't take my eyes off him.

I was so moved that I started to sing. That's when Eric opened his eyes. But then the prince's servant, Sir Grimsby, approached, so I hid behind a rock and watched them walk away.

Father's adviser, Sebastian the crab, suddenly appeared at my side. "We're going to forget this whole thing ever happened," he said.

Chapter Three

Later on, Daddy came into my secret cave. Sebastian had told him everything. Daddy was furious and lectured me about my responsibilities as a princess. But I didn't want to be a princess! I wanted to be a girl—a human girl.

Daddy ordered me to stay away from humans. I told him that I couldn't do that.

He lowered his trident and, with a single blast, destroyed all of my human treasures. When he left, I put my head down and cried.

Suddenly, I felt something brush against my arm. At my side were two eels that belonged to the sea witch, Ursula. "Ursula can help you," they hissed.

I had heard horrible stories about the sea witch, but I was so upset I didn't care. I just wanted to see Prince Eric again. I followed the eels to Ursula's cave.

Chapter Four

Ursula was very creepy. She offered to make me human for three days if I gave her my voice. She told me that I would stay a human if Prince Eric kissed me before the sun set on the third day. If he didn't, I'd belong to her!

I thought about what Daddy had said, but I was determined to see Prince Eric again. As soon as I signed the contract, my voice flowed into Ursula's seashell, which was tied around her neck.

At dinner, Prince Eric told me I looked beautiful. I smiled dreamily. It seemed like everything was falling into place.

The next day, Eric and I went out on his
rowboat. Eric stopped the boat in a lagoon.
There, he leaned over to me, and just as we
were about to kiss—*Splash!*

The boat flipped over! The kiss would have
to wait.

Chapter Six

I awoke on the third day, happier than ever before. But when I saw Eric, he was with another woman called Vanessa. I heard him say, "Our wedding ship departs at sunset."

I was crushed. Eric was going to marry Vanessa! I stared after them in astonishment. What had gone wrong? Now, I would have to return home as Ursula's slave.

I had been certain that Eric had the same feelings for me as I did for him, but now it was too late. I watched as Eric and Vanessa's wedding ship sailed into the distance.

Scuttle flew over. "I saw the bride in the mirror!" he squawked. "Vanessa is Ursula in disguise!"

So, now I understood—Ursula had tricked Eric into marrying her.

While Flounder pulled me out to the ship, Scuttle and some other sea creatures swam ahead and interrupted the wedding, dropping

things on Vanessa and spraying her with water.

When I got to the ship, I spotted the glowing
seashell that held my voice around Vanessa's
neck. Ursula had used my voice to make Eric
believe Vanessa was the one who had saved
him!

Scuttle snatched the necklace from Vanessa.
It fell to the ground and shattered, and my
voice flowed back to me. Then as loudly as I
could, I yelled, "Eric!"

"*You're* the one," Eric said quietly. "It was
you all the time!"

Eric leaned in to kiss me.

"It's too late!" Vanessa shrieked. The sun had just dropped below the horizon!

Suddenly, I changed back into a mermaid, and Vanessa became Ursula again.

Ursula took me to my father and showed him the contract. "I might be willing to make an exchange," Ursula told him.

Daddy agreed and took my place as Ursula's slave.

Chapter Seven

I had to do something to save Daddy and the kingdom, so I followed Ursula. She had used my father's trident to make herself monstrously huge. Then, she blasted Eric's ship and created a giant whirlpool. A wave struck Eric, throwing him onto a sunken ship that had floated to the surface.

While I distracted Ursula, Eric grabbed the wheel of the ship and steered the bow right into Ursula's cold heart. We had defeated the evil sea witch!

Daddy was free, and he forgave me for my selfishness. He also realized how much I loved Eric. He touched the water with his trident and transformed my tail into legs again! With his blessing, Eric and I were married and we lived happily ever after.